The Thanksgiving Blessing

Meadow Rue Merrill

HENDRICKSON PUBLISHERS   ROSE KiDZ

Lantern Hill Farm: The Thanksgiving Blessing

Copyright © 2019 Meadow Rue Merrill

RoseKidz® is an imprint of
Rose Publishing, LLC
P.O. Box 3473
Peabody, Massachusetts 01961-3473 USA
www.hendricksonrose.com
All rights reserved.

Book layout design by Talia Messina
Book cover by Drew Krevi
Illustrations by Drew Krevi

All Scripture quotations are taken from the Holy Bible, New Living Translation, copyright © 1996, 2004, 2015 by Tyndale House Foundation. Used by permission of Tyndale House Publishers, Inc., Carol Stream, Illinois 60188. All rights reserved.

ISBN: 978-1-62862-801-2
RoseKidz® Reorder #L50033
JUVENILE FICTION/Religious/Christian/Holidays & Celebrations

Printed in Dongguan City, China
Printed in April 2019 by RR Donnelley

To_____

From_____

Date_____

With heartfelt thanks for Roger and Patricia.

It is good to give thanks to the LORD.
Psalm 92:1

What was that wonderful smell? Molly sniffed once. She sniffed twice. Pumpkin pie! Today was Thanksgiving at Lantern Hill Farm.

Each year, aunties and uncles and grammies and grampies and neighbors and friends all brought something to share for Aunt Jenny's famous feast.

Thanksgiving was mashed potatoes!

Thanksgiving was turkey!

Best of all, Thanksgiving was a table full of tasty pies!

Molly bounced out of bed. Time to get ready!

5

"Over the river and through the woods, to Lantern Hill Farm we go," Molly sang on the way to the farm. "There's a barn full of hay and cousins to play and cups of hot cocoa!"

Cousin Jacob waited outside the farmhouse. Molly raced to join him.

"See what I made?" Jacob held up a pair of pinecone Pilgrim turkeys. "They are for the table. What did you bring?"

"Pie!" said Papa.

"Cranberry bread!" said Mama.

Even Charlie had brought
his smile to share.

But what could Molly bring?

She darted inside, hoping to find something quickly.

The kitchen burst with baked goods. Pots of yumminess bubbled on the stove.

Cousin Sammy stood by the counter. "See what I made?" Cousin Sammy pointed to a tray of popcorn ball turkeys. "What did you bring?"

"It's a surprise!" Molly shoved her hands in her pockets.

"It must be," said Sammy. "I can't even see it!"

Molly dashed down the hall, still searching.

The dining room sparkled with fancy dishes. Neighbor Rosa set a name card beside a napkin.

"See what I made?" Rosa said. "I wrote each person's name on the front so they'll know where to sit."

"Good idea." Molly frowned, wishing she'd thought of it.

13

Nothing to make.

How could Molly celebrate?

15

"What's wrong?" Aunt Jenny carried in a basket, followed by Jacob and Sammy.

Molly sighed. "Everyone has something to share for Thanksgiving except for me."

16

"Would you like to help pass these out?" Aunt Jenny held up a paper scroll tied with ribbon. "Then maybe you will think of something."

"What's inside?" Molly asked.

"A reminder of why we celebrate Thanksgiving," Aunt Jenny said. "Who knows why?"

"Because of the Pilgrims," said Jacob.

"Right," said Aunt Jenny. "The Pilgrims wanted to worship God in a land where they'd be free. So they left their warm, safe homes and sailed across the ocean on the Mayflower."

"Then they ate turkey and pie!" said Molly.

"Nope." Aunt Jenny laughed. "The Pilgrims were sick and hungry and cold. That first winter, many died. But the next spring, God sent Squanto and his Wampanoag friends to help them. They taught the Pilgrims how to plant corn and find food."

18

"That fall they had plenty to eat. The Pilgrims were so thankful, they invited their neighbors to a feast."

"With pie?" asked Sammy.

19

"Still no pie." Aunt Jenny laughed. "The Pilgrims didn't have wheat. They had pumpkins and squash from their gardens. They caught fish and dug clams. They roasted ducks and geese. And their new friends hunted for deer. Everyone brought something to share."

"Like us!" said Jacob.

20

"Exactly!" said Aunt Jenny. "Then they played games and feasted and sang for three whole days to celebrate God's blessings."

"Time to eat!" called Uncle Gerry.

If Molly didn't find something to share soon, Thanksgiving would be over!

The aunties and uncles and grammies and grampies and neighbors and friends marched into the dining room with steaming bowls of mashed potatoes, buttery beans, crisp corn, and tasty squash from Aunt Jenny's garden. The table groaned with fresh baked rolls, sweet-smelling bread, piping-hot stuffing, a giant turkey, and steaming pies.

Everyone had brought
something to share.

Everyone except Molly.

23

"Ready to open the scrolls?" Aunt Jenny asked.

Molly pulled the ribbon. Inside were words.

All people that on earth dwell, sing to the Lord with cheerful voice. Him serve with fear, His praise forth tell; come ye before Him and rejoice.

"Is this a song?" asked Molly.

"Yes," said Aunt Jenny. "One of the Pilgrims' favorites. Although they endured many troubles, the Pilgrims still found a reason to sing. When we go through trouble, we can sing, too. That's because a thankful heart will always find a way to say thank you. What are you thankful for?"

"That God sent friends to help the Pilgrims," said Jacob.

"For all this yummy food," said Rosa.

"For pie!" said Sammy.

"We all have something to give because we can all give thanks." Aunt Jenny smiled. "Now, who would like to share the Thanksgiving Blessing?"

"Me!" said Molly.

She had found something to share! Everyone bowed their heads, and Molly shared her thanks to God.

After dinner, Grampy picked up his fiddle, and everyone sang the Pilgrims' song together.

29

Thanksgiving is more than
turkey and mashed potatoes.

Thanksgiving is more than
a table full of tasty pies.

Thanksgiving is thanking God for his many blessings.

And that is something everyone can share!

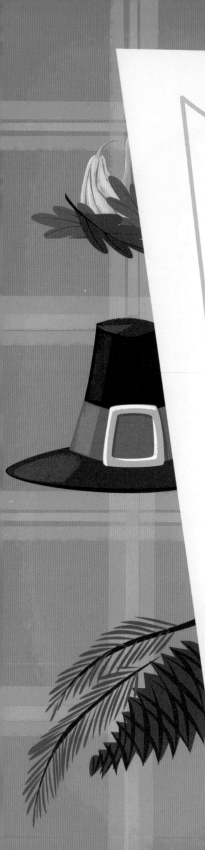

"The Old Hundreth," from Psalm 100, was one of the Pilgrims' favorite songs. It is sung to the tune we know as the "Doxology." To sing with the Pilgrims this Thanksgiving, help children print and decorate each verse of the song on a separate sheet of paper. Roll each paper into a scroll, tie with ribbon, and place one on each plate. Be sure to make one for each person, even if there are duplicates.

Old Hundreth

All people that on earth do dwell,
Sing to the Lord with cheerful voice.
Him serve with fear, His praise forth tell;
Come ye before Him and rejoice.
The Lord, ye know, is God indeed;
Without our aid He did us make;
We are His folk, He doth us feed,
And for His sheep He doth us take.
O enter then His gates with praise;
Approach with joy His courts unto;
Praise, laud, and bless His Name always,
For it is seemly so to do.
For why? the Lord our God is good;
His mercy is forever sure;
His truth at all times firmly stood,
And shall from age to age endure.
To Father, Son and Holy Ghost,
The God Whom Heaven and earth adore,
From men and from the angel host
Be praise and glory evermore.

For more from Meadow Rue Merrill, including other exciting ideas for celebrating God's love, visit her page on HendricksonRose.com